MUDDY WATERS
DUDLEY'S DILEMMA

I'M ONLY SMALL, AND SOMETIMES TINY. I'M ON EVERY PAGE, CAN YOU FIND ME?

Dudley was feeling very proud. He had been awarded the Golden Windlass for outstanding work on the canals around his home city of Birmingham.

He'd invited all his friends to the award ceremony. Even the Oxfordshire narrowboats were coming and he had a very special surprise waiting for them.

All narrowboats love chocolate. They've been carrying the ingredients around the waterways for hundreds of years. Their reward has often been a cargo of precious, golden chocolate coins. These have to be kept very safe so that Ol' One Eye, the pirate narrowboat, doesn't get them.

The coins are made at a secret factory in Birmingham. This is Dudley's favourite place in the whole world, but only the very best narrowboats are allowed to visit. Since his award of the Golden Windlass, he had permission to bring some close friends along, but there were very strict rules about how to get there.

There was great excitement at Thrupp, as the Oxfordshire boats prepared for their journey to see Dudley. 'Why has Dudley been given the Golden Windlass, Muddy?' asked Jolly Boatman.

'Well, Jolly, there are some boats who care far more about others than themselves, and Dudley is one of those extraordinary boats.' Jolly knew that Muddy Waters also had a Golden Windlass that he'd received long, long ago, although he never talked about it.

I'd really like to win the Golden Windlass one day, thought Jolly, as he puttered slowly out of the wharf. I wonder what I would have to do?

Dudley was waiting nervously for his friends to arrive. He was excited about taking everyone to the chocolate factory, but a journey with others was complicated. He knew all about the secret waterways. He had been through them many times, but always alone and always making sure he wasn't followed. He'd made a solemn promise that he'd never tell other boats how to get there.

He hoped the Oxfordshire boats would understand why they would need to wear blindfolds. After all, they wouldn't want Ol' One Eye finding out where the chocolate was made, would they?

Meeting at the Mailbox on the Birmingham Canal Navigation, everyone congratulated Dudley about the Golden Windlass. 'I really can't think why they picked me,' said a rather embarrassed, but still very proud, Dudley. 'The award ceremony isn't until later, so I've planned a very special treat for now. It's a visit to the chocolate factory!' he announced.

Everyone cheered and tooted loudly whilst Dudley quietly muttered, 'But there is one small problem...'

Leading from the front, Dudley towed all the boats in a long line. A few times around the Oozells Street Loop should confuse them enough, he thought.

'I'm not sure about these blindfolds,' complained Jolly Boatman, as he tried to peep through the bottom.

'Don't worry, Jolly, it won't be too far before we get there,' reassured Muddy Waters, who was also wearing a blindfold. He didn't like to tell Dudley that he'd been to the factory before and that he knew the way very well. It had been his treat, too, many years before when he was given the Golden Windlass.

Arriving at the chocolate factory, Dudley whispered that it was time for everyone to remove their blindfolds. Blinking and adjusting their eyes to the light, they all gasped as they saw the 'World of Chocolate' appear before them. They were greeted by Barney, one of the oldest chocolate factory boats. He winked at Muddy, remembering his visit from long ago.

'As you're Dudley's dearest friends, we've got some very special presents for you,' he said, as he released the first loading arm of golden chocolate coins.

Dudley was becoming a little anxious and tried to hurry everyone along. Although it was very exciting to be at the 'World of Chocolate,' he knew that he had to be at the award ceremony on time. Thanking Barney for their glistening goodies, they all headed off into the tunnels and canals of Birmingham.

Finding himself at the back of the group, Jolly decided he'd had enough of his blindfold and tow rope. He wanted to explore and see where he was going. This... was a terrible mistake!

Arriving back in the city, Dudley was preparing his big speech, when Muddy Waters asked, 'Where's Jolly? Wasn't he at the back?' Everyone looked around. Muddy had noticed that Jolly was very quiet on the return journey, but he thought that he must have been counting his precious cargo.

'JOLLY!!' they all called and tooted, but he was nowhere to be seen...

Jolly had drifted off into yet another tunnel. He was completely lost and was beginning to panic. He whistled loudly, hoping someone would hear him, but it was muffled in the dark, damp passageway. He didn't know whether to go backwards or forwards and wondered if he would ever see the other boats again.

He tried to remember what he'd been told to do if he got lost. He decided he'd 'stay still' once he reached the end of the tunnel. 'Surely my friends will find me,' he sobbed.

Dudley was in a spin. He knew everyone was waiting at the award ceremony, but he was very worried about Jolly. Muddy Waters seemed to know what Dudley was thinking. 'You go to the ceremony and we'll look for Jolly, he can't be too far away,' he said.

'But you don't know your way around these waters like I do, Muddy. There are more canals here than in Venice! Tell them to look after the Windlass for me,' shouted Dudley, as he sped off to find Jolly Boatman.

Dudley rushed through every lock and shortcut he knew, frantically searching for Jolly. He even sneaked through the barrier of one of the long abandoned tunnels, hoping that he could find his young friend. He tooted and whistled, but heard no reply.

Jolly emerged into the light of the late afternoon, realising it would soon be much darker. As he pulled into a nearby mooring, he heard a faint whistle at the end of the tunnel. Could help be on its way?

It was getting late and although everyone had waited patiently for Dudley to appear, some boats began to drift off. Muddy Waters, Poppy, Dizzy Spells, Cedric and Coal Face all looked anxious as the boats left the wharf. Bertie the Barge was in charge of the ceremony. He called Muddy Waters over and was about to ask him to look after Dudley's prize, when there was a sudden familiar whistle.

Dudley and Jolly hurried to the wharf, where everyone was so happy to see them. In the confusion, Jolly was bumped to the front and Bertie began his award speech, holding up the Golden Windlass.

'I don't think, that's for me, sir,' said a red faced Jolly Boatman, 'but if you don't mind, I'd like to be the one to give it to Dudley. I want to thank him for rescuing me,' he added, as everyone cheered Dudley on.

Glossary

Windlass: a large tool for opening lock gates

Narrowboat: a canal boat less than 2.1 metres wide that is steered with a tiller not a wheel

Cargo: things like wood and coal carried from place to place by the boats

Lock: gates on the canal which can be opened or closed to change the water level. Then boats can be raised or lowered as they travel through hills and valleys

Birmingham Canal Navigation: the network of many canals in and around Birmingham

Mooring: a space where the boats can stop and be attached to the canal bank with a rope

Wharf: a place where boats can stop to load and unload their cargo and where they can stay for a while

Other exciting Muddy Waters stories to enjoy

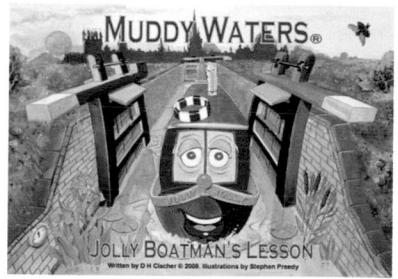

JOLLY BOATMAN'S LESSON
Written by D H Clacher © 2008. Illustrations by Stephen Preedy

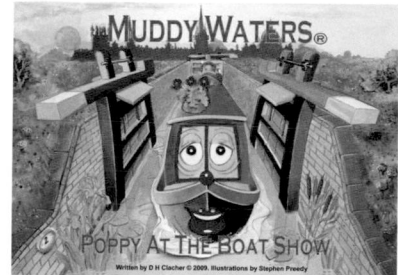

POPPY AT THE BOAT SHOW
Written by D H Clacher © 2009. Illustrations by Stephen Preedy

PEARLY'S WELCOME TO LONDON
Written by D H Clacher © 2009. Illustrations by Stephen Preedy

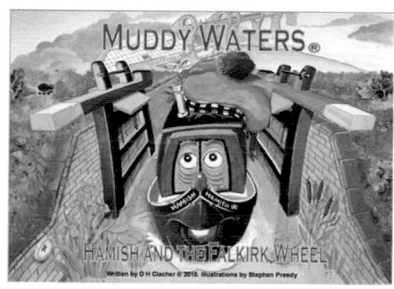

HAMISH AND THE FALKIRK WHEEL
Written by D H Clacher © 2015. Illustrations by Stephen Preedy

OL' ONE EYE'S REVENGE
Written by D H Clacher © 2016. Illustrations by Stephen Preedy

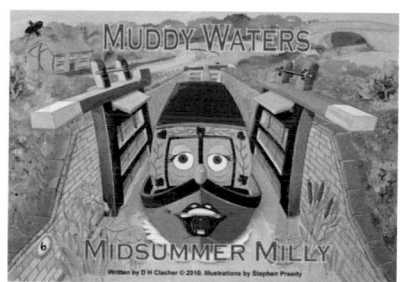

MIDSUMMER MILLY
Written by D H Clacher © 2010. Illustrations by Stephen Preedy

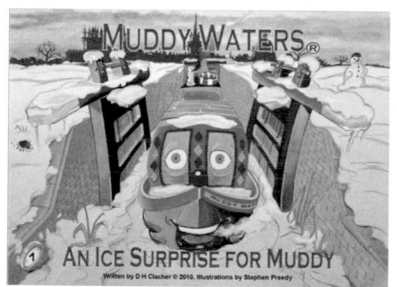

AN ICE SURPRISE FOR MUDDY
Written by D H Clacher © 2010. Illustrations by Stephen Preedy

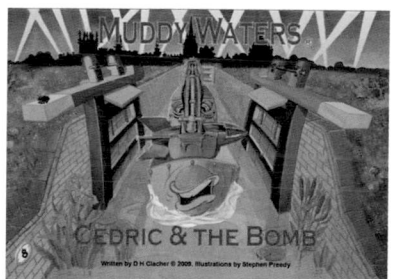

CEDRIC & THE BOMB
Written by D H Clacher © 2009. Illustrations by Stephen Preedy

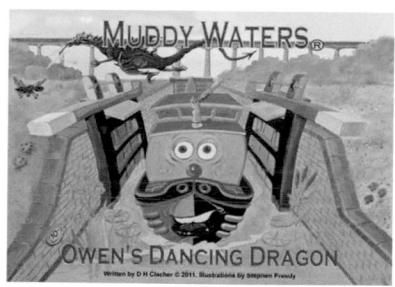

OWEN'S DANCING DRAGON
Written by D H Clacher © 2011. Illustrations by Stephen Preedy

www.muddywaters.org.uk..........

Stay **SAFE** near water -
Stay **A**way **F**rom the **E**dge

Go Wild Over Waterways - find games, learning and fun things to do at www.wow4water.net

Printed by Hunts (Oxfordshire) United Kingdom

Printed on FSC (Forest Stewardship Council)
paper which confirms that the product comes
from legal and well managed forests according
to strict environmental standards.

BIRMINGHAM

BANBURY

HEYFORD

THRUPP

Dudley's Day!